# MOUSE AND MOLE

## *A Winter Wonderland*

## WONG HERBERT YEE

sandpiper

HOUGHTON MIFFLIN HARCOURT

BOSTON   NEW YORK

To Margaret Raymo,
an editor for all seasons

The text of this book is set in Adobe Caslon.
The illustrations are litho pencil and gouache.

The Library of Congress Cataloging-in-Publication data is on file.

ISBN 978-0-547-34152-1 hardcover
ISBN 978-0-547-57697-8 paperback

Manufactured in Mexico
RDT 10 9 8 7 6 5 4 3 2

4500374452

# Contents

# Snug as a Bug

Mouse gazed out the window.

A snowflake drifted past.

Then another . . .

and another. Soon, it was

snowing like mad!

"Yippee!" yelped Mouse.

She rummaged through her closet.

Mouse pulled on snow pants.

Mouse tugged on

new boots: *thup, thup!*

She yanked a hat
over her ears.

She tied a scarf
around her neck.

Mouse buttoned her warm winter coat.
"Whew!" she exclaimed. "I am as snug
as a bug in a rug!" Mouse grabbed
mittens and rushed out the door.

Mole snuggled under the blankets.

"Bed is the place to be on

a day like this," he sighed.

"I am as snug as a bug in a rug!"

TAP-TAP-TAP.

Mole heard someone knocking.

He tugged the pillow over his ears.

TAP-TAP-TAP.

Mole still heard knocking.

"Open up, Mole. It's me,
Mouse!" called Mouse.

"Rats!" muttered Mole.

He rolled out of bed like a cocoon,

still wrapped in his blankets.

*Thump, thump, thump!* hopped

Mole across the floor.

He opened the door a crack —
*whoosh!* A gust of frosty air
nipped his snout.

"Morning, Mole!" said Mouse.

"Morning, Mouse," grumped Mole.

"Whatever are you doing out
on a day like this?"

"There is fresh-fallen snow!"
exclaimed Mouse.
"The trees are trimmed
with icicles. The bushes are
frosted like cupcakes.
It is a *winter wonderland!*"
she sighed.

"Your being out on a day like this makes

me *wonder* about you," Mole scolded.

"If you are not careful, Mouse,

you will turn into a *Mouse-cicle!*"

"Do not be silly, Mole. I am wearing

snow pants and a scarf. I have on

my hat and mittens too!"

"Your mittens do

not match," said Mole.

Mouse stuffed her paws

in her pockets.

"These are new boots," Mouse continued. "This is my warmest winter coat."

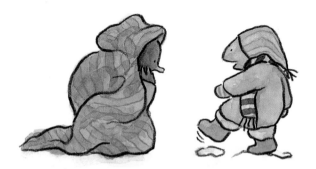

*Whoosh!* Another gust of wind sent a chill through Mole. "It is still f-f-freezing," he chattered. "Bed is the place to be — *bed* is the place for you and me!"

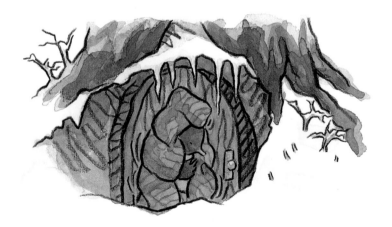

"But what about sledding?"
squeaked Mouse. "What about
snowmen and skating on the pond?"
"What about getting back
to bed?" grumbled Mole.
And *that* is exactly what he did!

# Sno-Mole

*ZOOM!* Mouse shot down the hill
on her sled. The sled hit a bump.
It flew up in the air.
"Yippee!" yelped Mouse.
*"Bumping–jumping on a sled,*
*better here than stuck in bed!"*
Mouse sighed. "Sledding is fun,"
she said, "but it would be more
fun if Mole were here."

She headed for the pond.

Mouse laced up her skates.

*Left, right, left, right!*

Mouse skated across the ice.

Mouse whirled!

Mouse twirled!

She made perfect figure eights,
forward and backwards.
*"Across the ice I zip and glide,*
*better here than stuck inside!"*
Mouse sighed. "Skating is fun,"
she said, "but it would be more
fun if Mole were here."

Mouse took off her skates.
Mouse dragged the sled back to
the oak. She stared at the tracks
in the snow. They were all from
her boots. "I am alone; alone is me."
Mouse made a snowball: *pat-pat-pat!*
She threw it against the trunk —
*SPLAT!* "Hmm, not too wet
and not too dry."

ZIP!

Mouse tapped her boot.

Mouse twirled her tail.

She came up with a plan!

It began with another ball of snow.

Mouse rolled it around the oak.

The snowball got bigger . . .

and BIGGER.

Mouse pushed it on the sled.

Then she went to work on the middle.

*Push and roll, roll and push!*

Mouse set the middle part on

top of the bottom part.

"Whew!" she huffed.

"Now for the head."

*Plink!* Mouse knocked an icicle
off the branch with a twig.
"Just the thing for a nose,"
she proclaimed. *Crack!* Mouse
snapped the twig in two.
"Now I have arms as well!"

Mouse used acorns for eyes and
pebbles to make a mouth.
She took a step backwards.
The snowman looked familiar.
The snowman reminded Mouse
of someone she knew. "I shall call
you *Sno-Mole*," she snickered,
"because you look just
like my friend!"

Mouse tapped her boot.

Mouse twirled her tail.

Something was still missing.

She headed back to the oak tree.

Mouse crept down the stairs . . .

and snuck into Mole's hole.

She rummaged through Mole's closet.
"Mole does not need a hat," whispered
Mouse to herself. "He does not need
his scarf or mittens either."
She tiptoed back outside.

Mouse put the hat on the snowman's head.
Mouse wrapped the scarf around
the snowman's neck. She stuck
mittens on the twigs.
Mouse looked at Sno-Mole.
Sno-Mole looked at Mouse.
"What about sledding?"
she squeaked,
"or skating on the pond?"

Mouse ducked behind the snowman.

*"Bumping-jumping on a sled?*

*What if I should lose my head?*

*Skating is something I would not miss.*

*Skating would be perfect on a*

*day like this!"* sang Sno-Mole.

And that is exactly

what they did!

# The New Friend

Mole huddled under the covers.

He was as snug as a bug in a rug.

Mole rolled to his left.

Mole rolled to his right.

Mole rolled right off the bed —

*whump!* He lay on the floor

like a cocoon in his blankets.

"I am as bored as a turtle in its shell.

I wonder what Mouse is up to?"

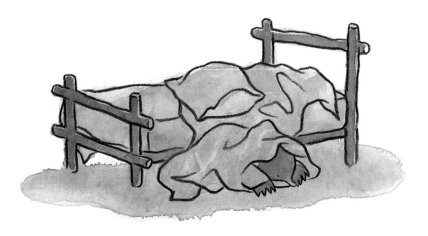

*Thump, thump, thump!* hopped Mole across the floor. He opened the door a crack — *whoosh!* A gust of frosty air nipped his snout. Mole saw Mouse headed down the path. Mouse was not alone. Someone was following his friend. "Yikes!" cried Mole. "Stranger danger!"

Mole rummaged through his closet.

He pulled on snow pants. He tugged

on boots: *thup, thup!*

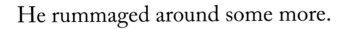

"Rats, no hat!"

muttered Mole.

He rummaged around some more.

"Phooey! No scarf or mittens either."

Mole buttoned his coat and ran outside.

He followed the stranger that

was following Mouse.

The tracks led Mole to the pond.
He ducked down in the cattails. *ZOOM!*
Mouse flew past with the stranger
in tow. "Yippee!" she yelped.

The stranger had a smile on its face.
Mole nearly toppled out on the ice.
"That is no stranger!" he gulped.
"Mouse is with a friend . . .
and that friend is not ME!"

*ZOOM!* Mouse and her partner zipped

by once more. Mole rubbed his snout.

Something about this new friend

was awfully familiar — *ZOOM!*

"Why . . . *that* is my hat!" said Mole.

*ZOOM-ZOOM!* "And *those* are my

mittens and matching scarf too!"

Mole watched in disbelief as

Mouse and her partner

made perfect figure eights,

forward and backwards.

Together, they skidded to
a stop. Mouse whirled!
Mouse twirled!

The new friend just watched.
"Hah!" Mole huffed. "Easy-peasy!"
He darted out onto the ice.
*Left, right, left, right!* tottered Mole
across the pond. Mole whirled!
Mole twirled! His arms began
to windmill.

Mole was out of control! "Gangway!"
he hollered — *WHAM!* Mole slid
*smack* into Mouse's partner.

OOF!

The snowman's
head toppled off.
It rolled across the ice.
Mouse stared at Mole.
Mole stared at the headless snowman.
"I am sorry, Mouse," mumbled Mole.
"I was showing off to your new friend."

Mouse could not help giggling.
"You do not have to be jealous
of a snowman," she laughed.
"Even if it does rather look like you!"
Together, Mouse and Mole put the
snowman's head back on top.

"Mole, meet *Sno-Mole*," said Mouse.
"Sno-Mole, this is Mole,
my neighbor and *best* friend."

Mole's face turned crimson like
winter berries. He gave Sno-Mole
a high-five. The twig arm flew off.
It skittered across the ice.
"Whoops!" said Mole.
He stuck the twig back in place.

"Br-r!" The frosty air
made Mole shiver.
"May I have my hat back?"
said Mole to Sno-Mole.

Mouse ducked behind the snowman.

"*I do not need a hat,*" squeaked Sno-Mole.

Mole stuffed his paws in his pockets.

"What about the scarf and
m-m-mittens?" he chattered.

"*I do not need a scarf.*
*I do not need mittens either,*"
giggled Sno-Mole.

"*They make me feel as snug . . .*
*as a bug in a rug!*"

Mole yanked the hat
on his head.

Mole tied the scarf
around his neck.

He tugged on mittens and grabbed
Mouse's paw. "What about skating?"
chuckled Mole.

Mouse picked up the rope to the sled.
Together, they circled the pond.
Mouse, Mole, and Sno-Mole
made perfect figure eights,
forward and backwards.
"Yippee!" yelped Mouse.
"Yahoo!" yelled Mole.
Sno-Mole just smiled.

# Sno-Mouse

*Dig! Dig! Dig!* Mole shoveled snow

from the door. *Scrape! Scrape! Scrape!*

He cleared the snow off the steps.

Mole spotted Sno-Mole in the yard.

Mouse's snowman seemed lonely.

Mole tapped his boot.

Mole rubbed his snout.

He came up with a plan!

It began with a ball of snow . . .

Mouse gazed out the window.

She saw Mole beside her snowman.

Someone else was down there too!

Mouse wondered who it could be.

Quickly, she pulled on
her snow pants and
tugged on her boots:
*thup, thup!*

Mouse yanked a hat over her ears
and wrapped a scarf around her neck.
She buttoned her coat,
found mittens that matched,
and rushed out the door.

"Surprise!" shouted Mole.

Mouse clapped her mittens in delight.

Mole had built a snowman of his own!

Mouse took a step backwards.

The snowman looked familiar.

The snowman reminded her

of someone she knew . . .

"Mouse, meet *Sno-Mouse*,"

said Mole, "Sno-Mole's neighbor

and best friend!"

Mouse could not help giggling.

She gave Sno-Mouse a high-five.

The twig arm fell off.

"Whoops!" said Mouse.

She stuck the twig

back in place.

"I'll be right back," said Mole.

He returned dragging something

through the snow.

"What about sledding?" Mole chuckled.

Mouse ducked behind Sno-Mouse.

Mole hid beside Sno-Mole.

*"Bumping-jumping on a hill?*

*What if we should take a spill?*

*You go ahead, enjoy the ride.*

*We'll be waiting, side by side!"*

sang Sno-Mole and Sno-Mouse.

And that is exactly what they did!

*ZOOM!* Mole and Mouse sped
down the hill. Mole and Mouse
hit a bump. The sled soared
through the air.

"Yahoo!" yelled Mole.

"Yippee!" yelped Mouse.

*Ker-THUNK!*

The sled crashed and flipped over.
Mouse and Mole tumbled
down the slope.

Snow crusted their hats!
Snow filled their boots!
Snow got into their
warm winter coats!
Mouse and Mole's
mittens were sopping wet.
Mouse shivered.
"I feel like a *Mouse-cicle.*"
Mole shivered. "I feel like a *Mole-cicle.*"
"Whatever are we doing out on a
d-d-day like this?" they chattered.
Together, they trudged
back to the oak.

Mouse and Mole huddled in front
of the fire. They wrapped themselves
in blankets like cocoons.

*Whee!* whistled the teapot.
*Thump, thump, thump!* hopped Mouse
and Mole across the floor.

Mouse took the teapot off the stove.

Mole fetched the cookie jar.

Mouse sipped. Mole nibbled.

Mouse nibbled. Mole sipped.

Together they sat gazing

out the window.

A snowflake drifted past.
Then another . . . and another.
Outside, the oak tree was
trimmed with icicles;
the bushes frosted
like cupcakes.
Mole sighed. "It is truly
a *winter wonderland!*"
he exclaimed.
Mouse could not
help giggling.